No Place for a
PIG

Text and illustrations copyright © 2003 by Suzanne Bloom
All rights reserved

Published by Boyds Mills Press, Inc.
A Highlights Company
815 Church Street
Honesdale, Pennsylvania 18431
Printed in China

Publisher Cataloging-in-Publication Data (U.S.)

Bloom, Suzanne.
   No place for a pig / written and
illustrated by Suzanne Bloom.
[32] p. : col. ill. ;   cm.
Summary: When a woman brings a pig back to
her apartment, she is faced with the challenge
of raising it in the city.
ISBN 1-59078-047-7
1. Pigs—Fiction. 2. City and town life—Fiction. I. Title.
   [E]   21   2003

First edition, 2003
The text of this book is set in 14-point Minion.
Visit our Web site at www.boydsmillspress.com

10 9 8 7 6 5 4 3

For Tom & Kathy, Jared & Molly
—S. B.

No Place for a
PIG

Suzanne Bloom

Boyds Mills Press

"Win a pig! Win a pig!" It was the voice of Radio Ray. "Can you name three famous pig tales?"

"Nothing could be easier," Ms. Taffy told her cats. She telephoned the radio station and said, "The Three Little Pigs," "This Little Piggy Went to Market," and "Charlotte's Web."

"Congratulations!" said Radio Ray, "your prize is waiting for you at Hog Heaven."

"Thank you," Ms. Taffy replied, thinking to herself, I have just the place for it on my shelf.

Then she grabbed her coat and some cookies and dashed downstairs. On the second floor she smelled Grandma Winona's simmering soup. There was always enough for everyone. On the first floor she heard hammering. Marcus and his friend Jubilee were probably working on another project. She couldn't wait to show them her prize pig.

Ms. Taffy had to take a bus and two trains. It was a long trip. But Hog Heaven wasn't hard to find.

"These are spectacular!" she thought, admiring the plastic pigs that filled the yard. "But too huge for my tiny apartment. The delicate little pigs must be in that shed." In fact, there was a note for her on the door.

"Dear Winner, We had to go pick up more pigs. Please pack up your pig in the case provided. Her name is Serena. Good luck!"

Rusty hinges squealed as she opened the door. Floorboards groaned underfoot. Tumbling over the carrying case, Ms. Taffy yelped, "Holy cow! You're a *real* pig!"

As the hay and dust settled, Ms. Taffy sat down to think. She shared an oatmeal cookie with Serena and said, "Now what?" Serena answered by walking right into the carrying case. They both grunted as Ms. Taffy lugged Serena back to the train station.

How hard can it be to feed a piglet? Ms. Taffy mused all the way home.

By the time they returned, the bakery was closed and so was the fruit stand. They scurried past the creaky fence in front of the vacant lot and tip-toed upstairs to Ms. Taffy's tiny apartment.

It was too late to introduce Serena to anyone but the cats.

The next morning, Ms. Taffy and Serena trotted around the corner to *Martha's Mouthful*. Serena slurped seven servings of corn flakes, munched a dozen corn muffins, and gobbled up eight ears of corn.

"Oh, my stars," Ms. Taffy sputtered, "I hope you're not this hungry every day."

But she was. So day after day they bought bags full of vegetables. They searched for spotty fruit and squishy squash because it was cheaper than perfect produce. It wasn't until the end of the week that they ran into their neighbors and Ms. Taffy finally introduced them to Serena.

"Isn't she beautiful?" Ms. Taffy said beaming. "The only problem is she eats like a pig."

Jubilee let her nibble a ragged cabbage leaf. Marcus fed her a cooked carrot. Grandma Winona stroked Serena's ears and said, "She looks a bit puny. Better come with us."

In Grandma's kitchen they pondered the problem over lunch. Between sips of steamy soup and bites of warm zucchini bread, Jubilee said, "Serena eats so many vegetables, you should grow them, Ms. Taffy."

Grandma smiled. "Grow a garden in the city?" she said. "Jubilee honey, you have a good imagination. But this little piggy needs a heap of greens now."

"But how are we going to haul them all?" asked Ms. Taffy.

Days later Marcus amazed them with a remarkable cart
that he had built.

"It's my own design," he said with pride. "I found the box
in the lot next door and my dad helped me put on the wheels."

Now they could go to markets all over the neighborhood, and collect a variety of vegetables. Every week or so Marcus and Jubilee adjusted the harness. But soon they ran out of strap.

Serena could no longer scamper up the stairs. Doorways and hallways were a tight squeeze.

"Ms. Taffy," said Jubilee. "Our pig's too big."

"She could move in with me," Marcus suggested. "My apartment's larger."

"Your parents would never go for that," Jubilee replied. "They already say your projects take up too much space. But maybe . . . we could build her a pig house."

"There's no place to put it," Ms. Taffy sighed. "I guess we'll just have to leave the city."

Early next morning, as Ms. Taffy started packing, she was startled by shouts from the street.

Marcus and Jubilee were hollering and pointing to the empty lot next door. "Serena . . . Ms. Taffy . . . a great idea . . . beautify our block . . ." was all they heard.

When they got downstairs Jubilee explained, "Grandma Winona got permission from the owner to clean up the lot and plant a garden, a vegetable garden! Marcus and I knocked on everyone's door and they all came out to help."

Neighbors were carrying out a mountain of junk. Marcus used the rickety old fence boards to build the pig house. Serena got right to work rooting in the dirt. Ms. Taffy planted seeds: peas, jalapeños, beets and beans, bok choy, broccoli, zucchini, and yams.

Over the summer the seedlings grew. Serena took mud baths and lazed in the shade of her sturdy new home. She watched the neighbors water and weed. She taste-tested the lettuce. Soon there would be enough crisp carrots, plump tomatoes, and eye-watering onions for soup, Serena, and all the gardeners.

Ms. Taffy had just come in from picking pea pods and was gazing down at the garden, when she heard the voice of Radio Ray say,

"Good morning fairy tale fans. Can you name three famous tales . . . about whales?"